This book is due for return on or before the last date shown below.

MUD BOY

A Story about Bullying

Sarah Siggs

With notes by Pooky Knightsmith

Illustrated by Amy Crosby

Jessica Kingsley Publishers
London and Philadelphia

First published in 2019
by Jessica Kingsley Publishers
73 Collier Street
London N1 9BE, UK
and
400 Market Street, Suite 400
Philadelphia, PA 19106, USA

www.jkp.com

Library of Congress Cataloging in Publication Data
A CIP catalog record for this book is available from the Library of Congress

British Library Cataloguing in Publication Data
A CIP catalogue record for this book is available from the British Library

ISBN 978 1 78592 870 3
eISBN 978 1 78592 871 0

Printed and bound in China

For my children and godchildren and everyone in between.
With special thanks to Pooky and all my love to John.

- S.S.

For my family: those I have gained and those I was lucky
enough to call mine from the very beginning.
Mud makes pretty mighty mountains.

- A.C.

Sam was so happy that he positively
bounced from one day to the next.

His smile was big
and his heart was full.

The sound of Sam's life was like the
best piece of music you have ever heard.

Sam had three
big sisters and
one small cat.

Sam's sisters liked
to ruffle his hair.

Sam *tried* to ruffle
his cat, but his cat
always ran off.

Everyone liked Sam, and Sam liked himself.

Sam's school was full to bursting with learning and laughter. Sometimes Sam missed being at home, but mostly he loved being at school.

His world felt right and Sam felt happy.

But then,
one Friday,
it began...

THE MUD

At first it wasn't too bad. Small
bits of mud came Sam's way and
he just pushed them off.

The mud didn't stick to him at all.

Just one girl was throwing it.

She aimed her mud words
at Sam's peachy cheeks.
"Go away, fat face!"

Then she aimed her mud
words at his bottom.
"Big bum, big bum!"

The other children giggled.

Sam giggled too.

But only on the outside.

Sam tried to keep away from the girl.

He moved towards his friends,
but his friends moved away.

Sam could hear whispering.
The girl was handing out mud
words for other children to throw.

A huge thud of mud hit the back of Sam's head. He tried to shake the words off, but the mud was sticky and it stuck.

Every day at school children waited for Sam.
They thought it was fun to cover him in mud words.
It wasn't fun for Sam. The soft, wet mud became hard
and dry, and Sam felt as if he was cracking. The mud
stopped him smiling. It stopped him talking. It clogged
up his ears, so he couldn't learn at school anymore.

The mud words were getting louder and bigger and pulling him down. Sam became heavier and heavier until he felt like he couldn't move and he couldn't breathe. The mud was getting inside his head. Even though people said good things to Sam, he couldn't hear them.

Nothing got through the mud.

The music had stopped.

Sam didn't know what to do. He got home from school and climbed into his wardrobe. He hugged his legs and closed his eyes. Now when Sam thought about school he felt sick and scared and his tummy hurt. He sat there for a long time. It was quiet and dark. The clothes smelt familiar and being curled up was comforting. Sam felt safe. He wanted to stay there forever.

At the far end of the wardrobe something moved. It moved slowly and quietly towards the sad and silent mud boy. A gentle tickle brushed along Sam's leg. Then he felt a soft nudge.

"Hello cat," sighed Sam, "I wish you could help me. I don't want to go to school anymore."

Some mud, at the corner of Sam's mouth, dropped off.

"I just feel like crying all the time."

The mud that was covering Sam's eyes fell away.

Sam put his arms around his cat.

"It helps when I talk to you!"

More mud came off, this time from Sam's fingers.

Sam ruffled his cat's fur...and his cat didn't run away.

His cat purred
VERY
LOUDLY.

Sam's mum heard the purring, and when she found Sam and his cat at the bottom of the wardrobe she got in too!

Sam's cat gave him another nudge, then stretched over his legs and left.

P PUURRR

Sam told his mum what was happening at school.

His mum listened.

"I've got mud words all over me.
I'm just a pile of rubbish!"

Sam's mum listened some more.

Then she said,

"Mud words can muddle your mind and
make you believe things that aren't true.

Now you've told me, we can begin
to un-muddle things together.

I love you Sam."

The heavy mud that was pushing down
on Sam's shoulders clomped to the floor.

Sam sat up tall...and his head disappeared up a jumper! He and his mum laughed and laughed.

At dinner, Sam told his three big sisters about the mud words.

The first one hugged him and wouldn't let go, the second one cried,

and the third one was so angry that she wanted to
hire a digger and dump mud on everyone at the school!

Dad calmed everything down.

Then he wrote to Sam's teacher, telling her
about the mud words and asking for some help.

Sam's teacher was *really* pleased with Sam for mentioning the mud. She told Sam that teachers can't always see the mud words, so it's always best to tell them.

Sam felt pleased too. He was beginning to feel much lighter and much brighter.

Then...something happened that Sam would never forget.

It was the middle of the day and as Sam bounced out to play with the rest of his class he saw something that made him stop.

He stood and he stared.

Running across the playground was a boy with mud words in his hair.

Then, Sam noticed a girl with
mud words on her shoes.

Sam hadn't known there were
other mud children.

He thought the mud words
only happened to *him*.

As Sam watched he noticed a boy
holding lots of mean mud words.

The boy slowly raised his arm
and took aim at the girl.

Sam ran as fast as
he could and jumped
between them.

He put up his
hand and shouted,

"STOP!"

The boy stared at Sam.

Sam stared back. He could feel
his heart beating-beating-beating.

Then, the boy dropped the
mud words and walked away.

Sam turned to the girl
and looked at her kindly.

"Don't worry," he told
her, "I know what to do!

And, by the way,
I *really* like your shoes."

The girl looked up at
Sam. Her smile was big.

Sam's heart felt full.

He knew he had done
something right and good.

Later that night, as Sam flopped onto his bed,
he felt sure that he could hear something.

He listened for a while...

and then he started
humming along.

The music
was back.

And it was the best piece of
music you have *ever* heard.

Mud Boy Guide for Supporting Adults
by Pooky Knightsmith

Mud Boy is a story that really captures children's imagination and gets them thinking about bullying and teasing. You will probably find that as you read it children will be full of questions, thoughts and feelings. Give them plenty of time and space to explore these ideas; if you feel comfortable doing so, let the conversation run freely and ask open questions to prompt thinking, such as:

- Can you tell me more about that?

- What do you think will happen next?

- How do you think that made him feel?

- Why do you think she did that?

- What might make things better?

- What might make things worse?

- What could he have done differently?

Where you can, try to reiterate the key messages from the book:

1. If you ask for help things will get better.

2. Other people might not realise what is happening if you don't tell them.

3. Bullying happens to other people too.

4. If you are bullied, it is not your fault.

5. You can make a difference if a friend is being bullied.

You can use a range of activities to explore any part of the book that feels especially relevant, for example:

- Choose an illustration and imagine what the people in the picture are thinking.

- Explore what would happen next if someone had said or done something differently.

- Describe what is happening in a specific picture in your own words.

- Think about what is happening from different points of view..

- Draw a picture that illustrates one of the important messages of the book.

Specific questions you can use to expand the learning from *Mud Boy* include:

Why do children in the book throw mud words? Is it Sam's fault?

Here we can explore how teasing and bullying start and how they can escalate. You can also consider what is okay, and what is not okay when it comes to banter and teasing and if these boundaries are different for the bully and the victim. It's important for children to realise that we are all capable of harming others with mud words but we can stop and be kind if we realise that we are making someone unhappy.

What are mud words and what other forms might they take in real life?

Think about the different forms that bullying can take. Explore whether some types of bullying are worse than others. The old saying goes "sticks and stones may break my bones, but words will never hurt me" - is this true? Think too about online bullying and consider how much easier it can be to throw mud words online when you can't see someone's face.

Should Sam throw mud words back? Why/why not?

Explore whether retaliation would have helped Sam. Think too about whether it's helpful if you retaliate on behalf of someone you really care about - maybe think about how one of Sam's sisters was "so angry that she wanted to hire a digger and dump mud on everyone at the school" and consider whether this would have helped or not.

How did the mud words make Sam feel?

Think about how things feel from Sam's point of view and how the mud feels heavier and heavier as the bullying goes on. Explore why this is and why at first Sam is able to ignore the mud words or laugh along, but after a while they really weigh him down and he wants to completely hide away from everyone.

What made the mud fall away? Why?

Think about when things started to change and why. Explore why Sam felt better when he talked to his cat and then his mum. Also think about the end of the book and how Sam's kindness made other people's mud fall away too.

Why didn't Sam tell anyone about the mud words right away?

Consider the different reasons why Sam might not have told someone. Perhaps he thought everyone already knew but just didn't want to help, or maybe he didn't think he'd be taken seriously, or he didn't want to worry anyone. Or maybe he thought the bullying would get worse if he got the bullies in trouble, or perhaps he just thought everyone was too busy to listen to his worries. During this conversation, be sure to reiterate the importance of seeking help, and the positive outcomes for Sam once he did open up, whilst acknowledging that it can be hard.

Who else could Sam have talked to?

Think about the different ways that we can get help if we are being bullied - it's important for children who might not feel able to confide in their cat and their mum, like Sam did, to know how else they can get support, and what will happen if they do.

How does Sam feel when he realises that mud words happen to other children?

Think about how alone Sam felt when he thought that he was the only one with mud words, and how differently he felt when he saw other children with mud words in their hair and shoes. You could also think about the part of the story where Sam told the girl with mud words on her shoes "Don't worry, I know what to do" - talk about what Sam did next to help the girl.

Whether you're reading the story with one child, or with many, try to give them time and space to explore the many ideas, thoughts and feelings that the story provokes. Try to enable them to feel safe and empowered to ask for help if they are bullying, being bullied or worried about a friend. Tell children that they can talk to you or another trusted adult if they are worried and let them know about the Childline website and helpline, which can be a brilliant support if they're not ready to confide in an adult face to face yet.

Visit the website at www.childline.org.uk or call 0800 1111

Read more kids' books from JKP!

Minnie and Max are OK!

978 1 78592 233 6

The Princess and the Fog

978 1 84905 655 7

Not Today, Celeste!

978 1 78592 008 0

Ellie Jelly and the Massive
Mum Meltdown

978 1 78592 516 0

Molly the Mole

978 1 78592 452 1

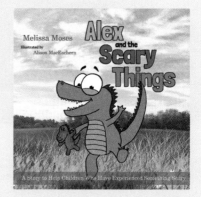

Alex and the Scary Things

978 1 84905 793 6